WELCOME TO
PASSPORT TO READING
A beginning reader's ticket to a brand-new world!

Every book in this program is designed to build read-along and read-alone skills, level by level, through engaging and enriching stories. As the reader turns each page, he or she will become more confident with new vocabulary, sight words, and comprehension.

These PASSPORT TO READING levels will help you choose the perfect book for every reader.

READING TOGETHER
Read short words in simple sentence structures together to begin a reader's journey.

READING OUT LOUD
Encourage developing readers to sound out words in more complex stories with simple vocabulary.

READING INDEPENDENTLY
Newly independent readers gain confidence reading more complex sentences with higher word counts.

READY TO READ MORE
Readers prepare for chapter books with fewer illustrations and longer paragraphs.

This book features sight words from the educator-supported Dolch Sight Words List. This encourages the reader to recognize commonly used vocabulary words, increasing reading speed and fluency.

For more information, please visit passporttoreadingbooks.com.

Enjoy the journey!

marvelkids.com

Little, Brown and Company

Hachette Book Group
1290 Avenue of the Americas, New York, NY 10104
Visit us at lb-kids.com

Little, Brown and Company is a division of Hachette Book Group, Inc.
The Little, Brown name and logo are trademarks of Hachette Book Group, Inc.

The publisher is not responsible for websites (or their content)
that are not owned by the publisher.

First Edition: October 2016

ISBN 978-0-316-27151-6

10 9 8 7 6 5 4 3 2 1

CW

Printed in the United States of America

Passport to Reading titles are leveled by independent reviewers applying the standards developed by Irene Fountas and Gay Su Pinnell in *Matching Books to Readers: Using Leveled Books in Guided Reading*, Heinemann, 1999.

MARVEL

DOCTOR STRANGE

I Am Doctor Strange

Adapted by R.R. Busse
Illustrated by Ron Lim, Andy Smith, and Andy Troy
Based on the Screenplay by Jon Spaihts,
Scott Derrickson, C. Robert Cargill
Produced by Kevin Feige
Directed by Scott Derrickson

LB

LITTLE, BROWN AND COMPANY
New York   Boston

Attention, Doctor Strange fans!
Look for these words when you read this book.
Can you spot them all?

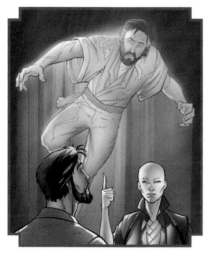

spirit

practice

explosion

cloak

This is Stephen Strange.

He is a doctor.

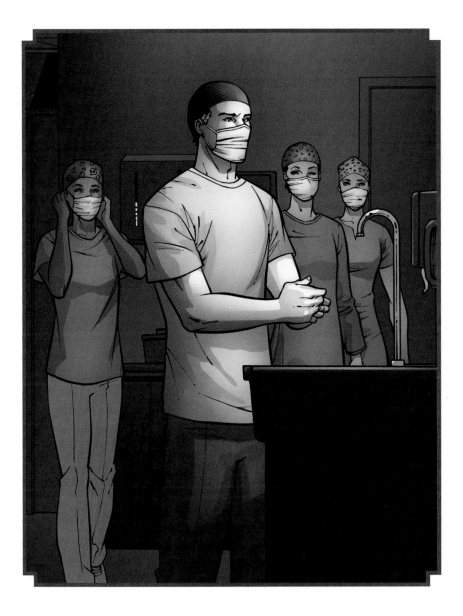

He helps sick people.

He is very good at his job.

One day, his car crashes and
his hands are very badly hurt.
He cannot be a doctor anymore.

Doctor Strange looks

for people to help him.

He travels around the world,
but nobody can fix his hands.
He is very sad, but he stops to
take care of a small dog anyway.

Someone is watching Doctor Strange!
He wears a cloak, and it is hard to
see his face.
Who is this person?
Will he be a friend
or an enemy?

He meets Mordo.

Mordo knows powerful magic.

Mordo leads Doctor Strange to an old city and introduces him to his teacher.

She is called The Ancient One.

The Ancient One teaches magic.
Nobody knows how old she is.
She is very quiet and very wise.

The Ancient One shows Doctor Strange
the Astral Plane.
His spirit floats above his body.

Magic is very weird.

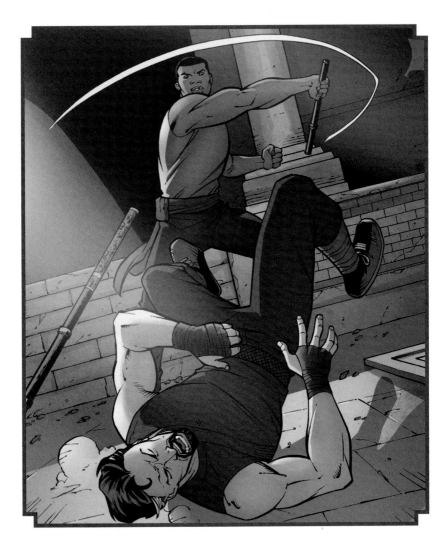

Mordo shows Doctor Strange how
to defend himself with magic.
They train for a long time.

Doctor Strange has a lot to learn.

He needs to practice to get better.

Mordo and The Ancient One show
Doctor Strange many portals.
Each portal goes to a different place.
Magic opens the portals.

Doctor Strange is still new to magic.
He cannot make his own portals yet,
but he wants to learn.
He will not give up!

Kaecilius used to learn from The Ancient One.

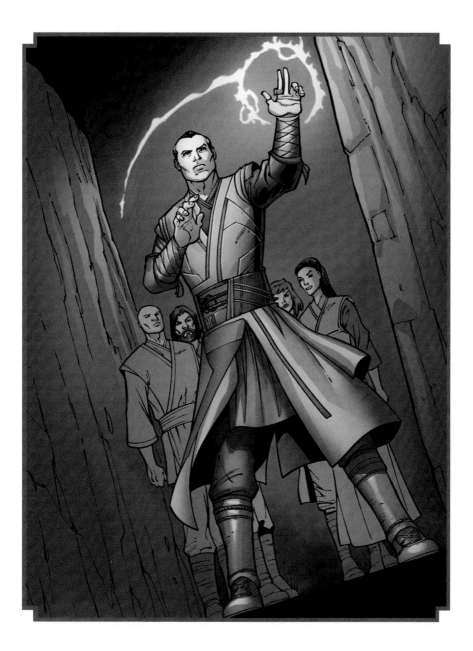

He wants even more magic.

His followers are called Zealots.

There is an explosion at
The Ancient One's school.
It is Kaecilius!
He is looking for a fight.

Doctor Strange escapes
through a portal.
It brings him to an old building
in New York City.
How odd!
Doctor Strange is very confused.

The building is called the
Sanctum Sanctorum.
Kaecilius and his Zealots
find Doctor Strange.
They attack!

Doctor Strange tries to fight,
but Kaecilius and his Zealots
are stronger than Doctor Strange.

Doctor Strange is losing.

But then he finds the Cloak of Levitation!

It is very powerful.

It protects Strange from punches and kicks.

Doctor Strange fights the Zealots with his new magic. Will he save the day?